DRAGON GIRLS

Stella the
...ragon

Maddy Mara

DRAGON GIRLS

Stella the Starlight Dragon

by Maddy Mara

Scholastic Inc.

This book is a work of fiction. Names, characters, places, and incidents are either the product of the author's imagination or are used fictitiously, and any resemblance to actual persons, living or dead, business establishments, events, or locales is entirely coincidental.

ISBN 978-1-338-84661-4

10 9 8 7 6 5 4 3 2 1   22 23 24 25 26

Printed in the U.S.A. 40

First printing 2022

Book design by Cassy Price

1

Stella woke to the sound of her alarm. She sat up, feeling confused. Was it time to get up for school? No, it couldn't be. Starlight shone through her bedroom window. Then she saw Rosie and Phoebe, asleep on sleeping bags on the floor. Stella and her two best friends had a sleepover most Friday nights, which meant that it was the weekend.

So why had her alarm gone off? And why was it shoved under her pillow, instead of sitting on her bedside table like usual? Stella quickly turned it off. The clock was shaped just like a star. Stella loved stars. Her name even *meant* star! But that wasn't the only reason she liked stars so much. Ever since she had been very young, Stella had wished on the first star she saw each night. Her favorite wish was always that something magical would happen.

Not so long ago, something *very* magical had happened. And not just to her but to her friends, too. The three girls had been transported into the Magic Forest, where they had become Night Dragons.

Stella was the Starlight Dragon, Rosie was the Twilight Dragon, and Phoebe was the Moonlight Dragon. Stella loved everything about being a dragon. She loved how powerful she felt. She loved roaring whirls of colored smoke that were deliciously and mysteriously cool. She also loved flying, even though she was still learning how to do it the right way.

So far, the Night Dragons had twice been summoned to the Magic Forest. Stella couldn't *wait* until they got called again.

The glowing numbers on her clock read 11:45 p.m. Suddenly, Stella remembered why she had set it in the first place. They were having a midnight feast! She fizzed with excitement as she pushed back the covers and stood up. The sleepover was at her house, so she was in charge of waking the others. Mostly, Sleepover Club was at Phoebe's house because she got homesick the most. But ever since they'd started going to the Magic Forest, Phoebe had become a lot braver. In fact, it had been her suggestion to have tonight's sleepover at Stella's place.

Her friends were still fast asleep as Stella knelt down beside them. "Rosie! Phoebe!" she whispered. "Time to wake up and FEAST!"

Her friends were awake in an instant.

Then Rosie smacked her forehead. "Oops! I left my treats in the kitchen. I'll go and get them now."

"I'll come with you," said Phoebe. "I put some juice in the fridge. Should I get glasses and plates while I'm there?"

"Good idea." Stella nodded. "While you guys do that, I'll set up a comfy spot for us here. Just be extra quiet so you don't wake my little brother!"

As her friends sneaked out of the room, Stella got busy. She pushed the sleeping bags to one side and grabbed the quilt off her bed. Her grandmother had made it. Little silver and gold stars had been embroidered onto fabric the color of inky-blue sky.

Stella smoothed it out like a picnic blanket on the floor. Then she collected all the pillows and arranged them around the edge. From under her bed she gathered her own offerings for the feast: popcorn and candy. Perfect! Stella stretched out on the quilt to wait for her friends to return.

Stella loved nighttime. She loved the velvety blue-black of the sky, and she loved how quiet

it was once the traffic died down and everyone was asleep. You could hear different things at night. Things that were drowned out by the bustle of the day.

In fact, Stella could hear something right now. What was it? She held her breath as a soft, beautiful song floated around her.

Magic Forest, Magic Forest, come explore…

The song was familiar. Stella smiled and her heart began to beat faster. This song meant that soon she and her friends would be returning to the forest. From the corner of her eye, Stella saw something strange. One of the stars on her quilt had just moved! She looked at the fabric more closely. An embroidered star shot across the quilt like a comet.

Magic Forest, Magic Forest, come explore...

Stella wondered if she should call out to her friends. But as quickly as she had the thought, she dismissed it. They always traveled into the Magic Forest separately.

Anyway, there was no time. The blue of her quilt floated into the air around her. Her bedroom walls began to fade away. A star shot past, sparking as it flew overhead.

Magic Forest, Magic Forest, come explore.

Magic Forest, Magic Forest, hear my roar!

Stella closed her eyes as she whispered the final notes of the enchanted song. Her stomach felt very strange, like she was falling and flying at the same time. But Stella didn't mind one little bit. She couldn't wait to return to the Magic Forest!

Slowly, Stella opened her eyes. She no longer felt like she was moving. Was she in the Magic Forest? It was dark, but Stella could see the outlines of trees. Long blades of grass swayed in a gentle breeze and the faint smell of tropical fruit wafted past.

Stella smiled. She was definitely back in the Magic Forest! She looked down. It was so cool to find herself transformed into a dragon. She was a deep purple and yellow, with stars on her wings. She would never tire of seeing her shining scales, strong limbs, and gleaming claws. But nothing was as awesome as her wings! Stella gave them a mighty flap, making the leaves on the nearby trees rustle and sending a ripple through the grass.

She breathed in deeply and let out a roar. Stella relished the sound of it echoing through the forest. The darkness lit up with a purple-and-yellow glowing light, creating a little patch of starlight that soon faded.

It was good to be back, but Stella had the feeling something was not quite right. Something was missing. She looked up at the sky and realized what was wrong. There were no stars! Sometimes the stars are hidden by clouds. And in the normal world, the lights of the city can make the stars hard to see.

But the sky above the forest was completely clear. And there were no city lights to cause problems here.

"This is not good," Stella muttered to herself, looking down with a frown.

In front of her was a small pool of crystal-clear water. Something in the water caught Stella's eye. A little golden starfish was lying on a rock. As Stella watched, it raised one of its five arms.

It's waving at me! thought Stella in delight. Carefully, she reached her paw into the water. To her surprise, the starfish jumped right into it! As Stella gently pulled her paw out of the water, the little creature gave itself a quick shake, water flying in all directions. Then it floated up into the air and began to turn cartwheels!

Stella blinked. A starfish with a funny little horn spinning in midair? This seemed like a very strange thing to see. *But this is the Magic Forest*, Stella reminded herself. She had seen plenty of weird and wonderful things here.

The golden starfish came to a stop in front

of Stella, bobbing up and down in the air like

it was floating in the ocean. Its friendly face

was smiling.

"Hi! I'm Stella," Stella said. She had no idea

who this creature was, but she was always

friendly when she met someone new.

The starfish did another spin. "I know," he said

in a surprisingly deep voice. "I'm LuckyStar, and I'm here to help you. Any questions?"

"So many!" Stella said. "Like, where have all the stars gone?"

LuckyStar twirled in the opposite direction. "That's a very good question," he said. "Unfortunately, I don't have a good answer. The truth is, no one is sure where they are. One night recently, there was a big flash. It was like the sky was on fire! It dazzled us all. When we could see again, all the stars had disappeared."

Stella frowned. "I bet it's the work of the Fire Queen," she muttered.

Stella and her friends had already dealt with

problems caused by the evil Fire Queen and her band of Fire Sparks.

"You're probably right," LuckyStar said, nodding the top point of his star. "That's why the Tree Queen has called you and the other Night Dragons to the forest. Come on! She's waiting for us in the glade."

Stella did not need to be asked twice. With a flap of her wings, she rose into the air. "Lead the way, LuckyStar!" she called.

The glowing star zipped off between the trees. He was very fast but easy to track in the dark, starless sky.

"You are flying really well!" called LuckyStar as they wove in between the trees.

"Thanks," said Stella. "I improve every time we come here. And on the first star I see each night, I've been wishing I'd get better at flying."

LuckyStar's glow seemed to falter. "That's one of the biggest problems now that the stars have vanished," he said. "No one can make any wishes. And without things to wish for, no one in the forest has anything to look forward to."

Stella loved making wishes. It would be awful if there were no stars to make them on!

She was about to tell LuckyStar not to worry, because she and her friends would get the stars back, when she spotted something bright up in the leaves of a tree.

Stella's heart leapt. Had they found a missing star?

She quickly decided this was not the case.
Gazing at the stars always gave her a warm
feeling. But she did not have that now.

"Watch out!" she called. "Fire Sparks!"

Stella was quickly surrounded by the pesky
creatures. The worst thing about Fire Sparks
was how they made you feel inside. In her
normal life, Stella sometimes got angry about
things, but the anger always passed quickly.

But the Fire Sparks really got under her skin.
When Stella and her friends had first come up
against the Fire Sparks, they'd tried to stay

calm. It was very hard! Getting mad seemed to give the Fire Sparks strength. Then over time, the Night Dragons had noticed something: They could use their anger to help fix things by channeling their feelings into action. And when they worked together, the sparks were no match for them.

Stella took a breath, ignoring the way the sparks stung at her skin and tickled her ears. She thought about the stars going missing. She was determined to get them back. There was no way these evil, electrified gnats would stop her and her friends!

With all her might, Stella roared, filling the air with purple and yellow. "OUT OF MY WAY!"

There was a fizzle, like a match being dropped in water. The air filled with a nasty-smelling smoke. When it cleared, there was not a single spark in sight!

Stella and LuckyStar did not meet any more Fire Sparks on their way to the glade. They soon reached the force field. It glowed with a honeyed light in the dark forest. Stella felt a surge of excitement. She couldn't wait to find out about their next quest.

She turned to LuckyStar. "Thank you for bringing me here," she said. "I hope we get to meet again."

LuckyStar did three quick cartwheels, sending out a trail of light. "I'm sure we will! I'll always be there when you need me," he trilled.

After one more cartwheel, he shot up into the sky, did a spin, then dove down into a nearby stream.

Eagerly, Stella pushed through the force field. On the other side, she couldn't see anything at all. It was so bright after the darkness of the forest! Stella blinked and her vision cleared. She sighed happily as she gazed around. The glade was always so perfect! Everywhere she looked were tiny glowing fruits and flowers. They twinkled as they moved in the breeze.

"Stella! You're here!"

Stella looked up when she heard familiar voices.

Rosie and Phoebe, in Night Dragon form, hovered nearby. Her friends landed on the plush grass and Stella was wrapped up in a three-dragon hug.

"How amazing is this?" Rosie exclaimed. "One minute we're getting ready for our midnight feast, the next we're in the Magic Forest! Do you think there's anyone else whose lives are as exciting as ours?"

Phoebe shook her head. "Not possible," she

said. "Hey, do either of you know what the quest is going to be? I guess it'll be something to do with the missing stars?"

"That's what I thought," Rosie said. "It's sad to look up and not see a single star in the sky."

The girls fell quiet as something moved in the center of the glade. The huge, elegant tree swayed from side to side.

"The Tree Queen is coming!" Stella exclaimed as the trunk of the tree transformed into a beautiful moss-green gown. The fluttering leaves turned into flowing hair framing a wise and noble face. Two branches reshaped into long arms, which the Tree Queen now held out in welcome.

"It is so good to see you, Night Dragons," the Tree Queen said in her strong, warm voice. "The Magic Forest needs your help."

"To get the stars back?" Stella asked. "I'm sure we can do it!"

The Tree Queen smiled. "It is good to be confident, Stella. It will be a challenging quest, though. Things have become more dangerous since your last visit."

"What's happened?" asked Phoebe.

Stella could tell that her friend was worried.

"The Fire Queen herself has been spotted in the Magic Forest," explained the Tree Queen. "Up until now, she has stayed out of sight. The fact that she has let herself be seen means that she is growing bolder."

"I guess that means she's getting more pow-erful, too?" Stella asked.

The Tree Queen nodded. "We don't know why she has stolen the stars. But until we have them back, none of the forest creatures can make wishes."

"And that means they have nothing to look forward to, right?" said Stella, remembering what LuckyStar had said.

"That's a big part of the problem," agreed the queen. Her voice dropped. "But it is even more serious than that. Wishes in the Magic Forest can actually change the future. Without wishes, we simply don't know what will happen."

Stella, Rosie, and Phoebe exchanged a look. This sounded bad.

Stella flapped her wings and rose into the air. "We'll fix this," she said. "I'm ready!"

The Tree Queen smiled again, although not

quite as broadly as usual. "It's important to be so enthusiastic," she said. "Let me tell you a few things first."

Stella landed on the ground with a bump, feeling silly. Sometimes she was just a little *too* keen to get things started. But a smile from her friends helped her embarrassment fade. She, Rosie, and Phoebe had quite different personalities, but they worked beautifully as a team.

"Stella," said the Tree Queen, "I'd like you to take the necklace. You will lead this quest."

She extended a branch-arm toward Stella. Dangling from it was a silver chain. On the chain was a tiny ball of magical thread. Although the thread had been used in their other adventures, it never seemed to get any smaller.

I wish tubs of ice cream worked like that, Stella thought.

"Where should we look for the stars?" Rosie asked. "Do you have any clues?"

The Tree Queen swayed. "Unfortunately not. The stars disappeared without a trace. One minute they were there, and the next they had vanished."

This was going to make their quest very difficult. The Magic Forest was a vast place!

"I suggest you start by visiting the Star Fields. There is a dance academy there, where the forest's stars are trained."

"Trained?" Stella laughed.

The Tree Queen nodded. "Twinkling and shining is not as easy as it looks. It takes a lot of lessons before a star is ready to join the others in the night sky. If you go to the Star Fields, you might find some clues. But the Fire Queen is almost certainly watching. Be very, very careful."

The Tree Queen turned into a solid tree once more.

This would be the most difficult quest the Night Dragons had been on. *But we'll do it,* Stella told herself.

She flapped her wings and rose into the air again. This time, Rosie and Phoebe joined her.

"Come on, Night Dragons!" Stella roared. "Let's go find us some stars!"

Stella, Rosie, and Phoebe flew through the shimmery force field and out into the Magic Forest. They flew higher and higher, until they were way above the treetops. Stella preferred flying very high. There were fewer things to crash into! The darkness closed in around the Night Dragons, but this didn't bother them.

Their eyes were perfectly adjusted to seeing in low light.

"I guess the stars in the Magic Forest are totally different from the stars in our world," Rosie commented as they flew. "I've looked at stars through my cousin's telescope. They're not normally something you could hide."

"I was thinking that, too," said Stella. "The sun is a star, after all. That would NOT be easy to steal."

"Which way to the Star Fields?" Rosie asked.

As Rosie spoke, the little ball of thread around Stella's neck begin to unwind. The end of the thread rose, just a little. It was pointing toward the horizon.

"I guess we go that way." Stella pointed.

She flapped her wings harder, loving the feeling of the cool night air rushing past. Stella wasn't perfect at flying yet, but that didn't stop her from loving every moment of it.

Phoebe swooped alongside her, wobbling a little as she tried to straighten up her wings. She scanned the forest below.

"Watch out!" Stella laughed. "You nearly crashed into me."

Phoebe also had a little bit to learn when it came to flying. But like Stella, she was improving every time they visited the forest.

"Sorry!" Phoebe said, swerving away. "I got distracted by that glow down there. Can you see it? Between those trees. It's pale. I am not sure if I'm imagining it."

"You're not imagining it," said Rosie, flying closer.

Stella felt the ball of thread give a gentle tug, and when she looked, the end of it was pointing toward the pale glow Phoebe had noticed.

"Here goes, Night Dragons," said Stella, taking a deep breath. "Get ready for landing."

The three friends flew lower and lower. Soon they were flying between the trees. The strange glow grew brighter. Stella stretched out her paws to brace herself for landing. It was about to be the best one she'd done, except that she bumped into a tree right at the end.

"I swear that tree wasn't there just before." Stella groaned, picking herself up.

Rosie laughed. "Yep, it just jumped into your way at the last minute," she teased.

"Anything is possible around here," Stella said.

Phoebe, who had landed near a dense row of trees, pressed a talon against her mouth in a silent shushing motion. With the other paw she beckoned them over. Stella and Rosie crept closer. On the other side of the trees was a strange sight.

Dozens of tiny star-shaped creatures were

lined up in rows. Their points were sharper than LuckyStar's, so Stella knew they were not starfish.

"They look like the sort of stars you draw!" Stella whispered in delight.

"I know, right?" Phoebe whispered. "Or like star-shaped cookies."

"Do you think they are the missing stars?" Rosie asked.

"Maybe," Stella replied.

Phoebe moved a branch to get a better look. "What are they doing? Having a dance class?"

Rosie nodded. "I think so. And that must be their teacher."

In front of the little stars was a small pink pony with a glittery, golden mane. She stood on her back legs and clapped out a rhythm with her shiny pink front hooves.

"Right now, junior stars. Five, six, seven, eight! And float to the left. Then twinkle! And float

to the right. Then twinkle!" neighed the pony. She tossed her mane and pranced around.

The junior stars did their best to follow the pony's moves. But they kept making mistakes. Some of them twinkled when they were supposed to be floating. Some floated when they were supposed to be twinkling. They kept crashing into one another.

"Now spin!" called the pony.

The junior stars tried to spin, but most of them lost their balance and ended up in a heap on the ground.

A big, dragon-y laugh burst from Stella. It was impossible to hold back. The little stars were adorable! Plus, it was nice to know she wasn't the only one who fell over when trying to do tricks.

The stars stopped dancing and turned toward the Night Dragons. The pony trotted over on her hind legs and pushed back the branches of the trees.

"Are you *spying* on us?" the pony whinnied. "No trespassing! This is the Star Fields Dance Academy!"

Stella's heart leapt. The Star Fields! So they were in the right place.

"We're not spies," Stella explained. "We're Night Dragons. We've been sent by the Tree Queen to find the missing stars. Are these little ones okay?"

"As you can see, they are fine," snorted the pony. She tossed her mane. "I am training them for a very important show. As you say, all the bigger stars have vanished. So I am trying to get this group ready to fill in."

The pony sighed dramatically. "I am a show pony, so I am very good at getting stars ready for performances. But they are a long way off! There is only so much I can do." The pony gave another sigh and pressed the back of a hoof to her forehead. "They just aren't motivated. The fiery lady will be cross. She wants the juniors to shine."

Stella froze. "Fiery lady? Who is that?"

"The one organizing the talent show." The show pony shrugged, as though it was not important.

"She's really scary!" shuddered one of the junior stars.

It *had* to be the Fire Queen. What was this talent show? But when Stella tried to ask more questions, the show pony swished her golden mane, sending glitter flying.

"Alas! There's simply no time for questions," she neighed. Pivoting back to her students, the pony clapped her hooves loudly. "Back into your rows! Once more, from the top."

But Stella had no intention of giving up so

easily. She pushed through the trees and into the clearing. Her friends followed.

The junior stars looked up at the three dragons, their eyes wide with amazement.

"I am sorry, but this is *really* important," Stella said to the show pony. "Can you please tell me more about the performance?"

The pony swished her tail. "I only give that kind of information to our students. It is a competition, after all."

"Okay," said Stella, thinking fast, "how do you become a student?"

She was getting annoyed. Couldn't the teacher see they were on an important quest? The safety of the junior stars was at stake.

Suddenly, all the little stars clustered around Stella. "You have to audition!" they called in their funny, tinkling voices. "You and the other dragons, too! Show Madame Prancey what stars you are."

"What should we do?" Phoebe whispered nervously.

"We don't know how to be stars!" Rosie added.

"I hardly know how to be a dragon," Stella agreed. "But I suppose we'll figure it out."

"Right. It's too important not to try," Phoebe said.

Stella could tell Phoebe was still worried. She was proud of her friend for not letting that stop her. Together, the three Night Dragons turned to face Madame Prancey.

"We will audition," said Stella, trying to sound more confident than she felt.

Madame Prancey snorted. "This is a dance school for stars, not dragons."

"But we are *Night* Dragons," said Stella. "And I am the Starlight Dragon. So I am a star ... kind of."

Madame Prancey thought about this, then nodded. "Fine. I will make an exception. This once."

The junior stars cheered and flocked around

the dragons. They seemed excited to see the audition. Or maybe they were just happy their lesson was over!

Madame Prancey shooed them back. "Give the dragons plenty of room," she warned. "If you get stomped on, you'll end up as stardust."

The little stars squealed and scattered.

Madame Prancey clapped her hooves once more. "Let us begin. To be allowed into the Star Fields Dance Academy, there are three basic moves you must be able to do."

Stella gulped. "What are the moves?"

"Twinkling. Shining. And shooting across the sky," Madame Prancey replied. "You can choose the order."

"We'll start with shooting across the sky," Stella decided, tingling with excitement.

This seemed like a move they would have no trouble with. She glanced at her friends. "Ready, on the count of three? One, two, three . . . go!"

Stella shot up into the air, Rosie on one side and Phoebe on the other. The three had flown together a lot, and they streaked across the sky in perfect formation.

"Go, Night Dragons!" whooped the junior stars.

"Loop?" Stella called, and with their wings stretched out to touch, the trio executed a neat loop.

When they landed, the little stars clustered around them, twinkling wildly.

"Not bad," Madame Prancey said. She looked surprised and impressed. "What will you do next?"

Stella looked across at her friends. Their bright scales were lit up by the glow of the small stars. "We're already doing the next one," she said, stretching out her wings. "Look at how we're shining!"

Madame Prancey tapped a hoof to her mouth thoughtfully. "That is true," she said. "You have a different type of shine, but you are definitely shining."

Stella grinned. They had already passed two moves!

Madame Prancey crossed her front legs over her chest. "Now it's time for twinkling. For stars, this is easy. They can twinkle in their sleep. In fact, they often are asleep when they twinkle. But I have never seen a dragon twinkle."

"We are not normal dragons, remember," Stella said. She turned to the others. "Let's try roaring," she said.

"That's not really twinkling," Phoebe whispered.

"Our roars are a bit twinkly, especially as they start to fade." Stella shrugged. "It's worth a try, right?"

Rosie and Phoebe agreed. The trio breathed in the cool night air and roared as loudly as they could. The sky above the clearing filled with swirling pinks, purples, blues, and oranges, lighting up the surrounding trees and making them glow.

"Oooooh!" The little stars clapped their points. "So pretty!"

"Very pretty, yes," Madame Prancey agreed, tossing her mane. "But not twinkling."

Stella frowned. "Why are you making this so hard?" she snapped. "We are trying to help the stars and the Magic Forest. Don't you understand that the Fire Queen is dangerous?"

Stella expected that the teacher would

argue right back. But Madame Prancey didn't say a word. She was looking at something just behind the dragons. The junior stars had also gone quiet.

Stella heard a voice. It was a crackling, harsh voice that felt like it was burning her ears. "You Night Dragons are really not very *bright*, are you?"

"She's back!" squealed the junior stars.

Heart thumping, Stella spun around.

Dry leaves and dust whirled around like in a sandstorm. As they watched, a figure loomed in the middle of the swirling mass. Long tendrils of golden hair glowed and flickered like candlelight. Ribbons of smoke rose from the figure's fiery dress.

There was no doubt who this was.

"The Fire Queen," the Night Dragons said in unison.

The Fire Queen swished an arm and the air filled with Fire Sparks. The heat was intense.

The junior stars shrieked and ran behind the dragons for protection.

"Pony, are these stars ready to perform?" the Fire Queen asked Madame Prancey, rising higher into the air.

"Th-th-they are improving," Madame Prancey stuttered. She trotted nervously on the spot. "But they need more time."

"There is no more time!" the Fire Queen roared. The heat of her breath made the leaves wither and fall from the trees. "The talent show is about to start! They must perform."

"We know you're up to something!" Stella yelled, finding her voice. "We're not going to let you steal the junior stars. The Magic Forest needs them!"

The Fire Queen glared at her with burning eyes.

Stella glared back. There was no way she was going to show her fear.

"I want the stars," the Fire Queen growled. "And what I want, I get." She stretched out her arms and Fire Sparks appeared.

"Watch out!" Stella warned her friends. "They'll going to grab the little stars."

The stars squealed and leapt onto Stella's back.

But the sparks did not grab the little stars. Instead, with a whoosh, they shot up into the sky.

The Night Dragons gazed up at the sparks. They swirled through the sky, arranging themselves into different shapes and patterns.

First, they formed a huge rectangle. Then they began to form words.

Tonight Only!

Magic Forest Talent Quest.

Only true stars may compete.

Show starting soon. Do not be late!

"See?" the Fire Queen cackled meanly. "I am simply here to let everyone know about the talent quest."

Much to the astonishment of the Night Dragons, the Fire Queen and her sparks flew off into the night sky. They didn't take so much as a blade of grass with them.

"Weird," Rosie said.

"Really weird," Phoebe agreed. "What is she up to?"

Stella had no idea, but she knew one thing for sure: There was no way the junior stars should go anywhere near that talent quest!

Madame Prancey trotted over. "I suppose that decides it." She sighed.

"Decides what?" Stella asked.

"You dragons will have to take the junior stars to the competition," Madame Prancey snorted. "I was going to take them. But I can't fly. We won't make it in time."

Stella stared at her, aghast. "You can't be serious! The talent quest is a trap."

"The Fire Queen is definitely up to something," Rosie added.

But Madame Prancey dug in her hooves.

"They must go," she said. "True stars always perform. No matter what!"

The junior stars twinkled furiously, jumping up and down on Stella's back. "We want to go! It's our first performance!"

"It could be your last one," muttered Stella under her breath. Doing what the Fire Queen asked seemed like a very silly idea.

Phoebe nudged her. "Maybe we should go," she said. "It's the only way to figure out what the Fire Queen is really up to. And we still need to find the missing stars."

"Phoebe's right," Rosie said. "And if we're *expecting* the Fire Queen to trick us, then she won't be able to. We're too smart for that!"

Stella smiled at her friends. She often felt like the brave one of the group. But her friends were every bit as brave as she was! "Let's do it. But we must be on guard at all times."

"For sure," Phoebe said.

Rosie began to giggle. "I can't believe I'm laughing when we've just met the Fire Queen. But you look so funny, Stella. You really ARE the Starlight Dragon."

All the junior stars were clinging to Stella.

"It's why we love you so much," trilled one of the little stars.

Stella smiled. She had always adored stars. Clearly, they adored her right back!

She made herself make a serious face.

"You must listen to me and my friends. Understood?"

"Yessssss!" chorused the stars.

"Do any of you know where this talent show is being held?" Stella asked.

"Noooooooo!" chorused the stars.

Madame Prancey did not know, either.

Stella frowned. The further they got into this quest, the more complicated it became.

She scrunched her eyes shut and let out a long, slow breath.

"Stay calm," said a familiar voice. "Losing your cool is not going to help right now. And remember, you're not doing this alone."

She opened her eyes to see LuckyStar spinning by her side. Phoebe and Rosie were also right there.

"We'll figure it out," Phoebe said.

"Together," Rosie added.

Stella felt a gentle tug. The ball of magical thread was unwinding. Its end pointed toward the horizon.

"That's the way to go," Phoebe said.

Stella nodded. "Hey, stars, can some of you please climb onto Rosie and Phoebe? I can't take you all."

"We want to ride on you!" they wailed.

Rosie laughed. "Nice try, Stella."

Stella sighed. The stars were very cute and very persistent. "Okay, okay! But you'll have to climb up onto my back rather than cling to my wings and legs. I can't fly like that."

The stars did as they were told and arranged themselves into neat rows.

"You look like a bus for stars!" Rosie laughed.

"I *feel* like a bus for stars." Stella grinned. "Let's follow those sparks."

"Goodbye, Madame Prancey," the junior stars called as Stella lifted up into the air.

Madame Prancey dropped onto all four legs and cantered along below them, calling up instructions as they flew off. "Remember! Float to the left first. And make sure you twinkle ALL your points, not just the top ones. And smile! A smiling star is a brighter star."

The Night Dragons flew above the night-cloaked forest, LuckyStar sticking close by. The stars on Stella's back sang endless rounds of "Twinkle, Twinkle, Little Star," but Stella hardly noticed. She was deep in thought about what lay ahead of them. The talent quest was definitely some kind of trap. They would have to be very careful.

Rosie looked over at Stella. "Notice how cold it's getting?" she asked.

Stella hadn't noticed, but now that she thought about it, it was very cold! The little stars began to shiver, sounding like wind chimes as they clinked against one another.

"Look!" Phoebe cried.

The trees below were covered with snow. The river wending its way through the forest was filled with big chunks of ice.

Up ahead, Stella saw something that made her forget the biting cold. A bright arrow loomed in the sky. It pointed down at something that glowed on the horizon. It almost looked like the sunrise.

But that made no sense. It was the middle of the night.

As they flew closer, Stella saw it wasn't the sun. It was a giant stage, held up by more Fire Sparks than Stella had ever seen. And floating in midair above the stage was the Fire Queen.

Her gown blazed even brighter as her magnificent fire-hair leapt around her.

She stretched out her arms, and when she spoke, her voice filled the air. "It is time for the first ever Magic Forest Talent Quest to begin!"

The animals of the Magic Forest were all gathered around the stage, cheering loudly. The Night Dragons landed and looked around in wonder. LuckyStar settled on Stella's shoulder.

There was a buzz of anticipation in the air. The little stars on Stella's back fluttered with nerves as they looked around. Animals lined the ground in front of the stage. Others perched in branches of trees, or bobbed in the river. More animals hovered overhead. The air was filled with the sounds of all the different creatures, jostling to get closer to the stage. More animals were arriving at every moment.

Two rabbits with neon tails hopped by. "Finally, something exciting is happening!" said one.

"Isn't it wonderful?" agreed the other. "Since the stars disappeared, life has been so dull. I don't feel like doing anything."

Up onstage, the flames around the Fire Queen burned like a bonfire warming everyone nearby.

"Creatures of the sky, land, and water. I am the Fire Queen!" she said in her crackling voice. "You may have heard about me. Bad things, no doubt. But this talent quest is my way of showing you who I really am. It is time for some fun, wouldn't you agree?"

"We certainly do agree," bleated a sunset-colored sheep who was standing with her flock. Everyone in the audience seemed excited. Everyone except the Night Dragons.

"I have such a bad feeling about this," muttered Stella. She just wished she knew what to do.

The Fire Queen smiled as she gazed across the crowd. "Who will be first to perform? It is a magical stage, so it will change to suit your needs when you step up here."

"We will!" chorused some gruff, furry-sounding voices. A group of badgers dressed in little velvet vests hopped up onto the stage. "We're the Beat Badgers," they announced. "We don't normally perform for others, but we are making an exception tonight. We just need a drum."

The Fire Queen swished her arm and a drum appeared at center stage. One of the badgers waddled over and began to thump it rhythmically. The rest of the badgers gathered round and began to make strange, growly noises.

"Is that *singing*?" Stella whispered, trying not to laugh.

"It's a bit hard to tell, but I think so," Rosie said, giggling. "They are very sweet, but their voices aren't great."

"It probably sounds lovely to other badgers," kindhearted Phoebe suggested.

However, it did not sound lovely to the Fire Queen. After a few seconds of the growly singing, she stopped the performance. "You are wasting my time. Clearly, you are not stars!" she snapped, and the Fire Sparks shooed the badgers off the stage.

"*Clearly*, you don't know talent when you hear it," huffed the drumming badger. He put his pointy nose in the air as he was hurried off.

Next onstage was a group of sparkly, silver-white bears. They were dressed in tutus and elegant scarves.

"They're wearing ice skates!" Stella said in surprise.

"They're the Gliding Bears," explained

LuckyStar. "They are famous performers in the Magic Forest."

"How will they skate on a stage?" Rosie asked.

But just then, the surface of the stage transformed into a smooth layer of ice. The bears began to move across the gleaming ice. They twirled and spun. They were strong and very graceful.

The crowd was impressed, clapping after a particularly difficult leap.

But the Fire Queen soon stopped them. "No, no, NO!" she roared, her flames flickering menacingly as she sent the bears offstage. "You're not right at all."

Stella was shocked. "What is she talking about?" she said to her friends. "Those bears are really talented!"

"Shhhh!" warned LuckyStar, spinning with worry.

The Fire Queen turned to glare at the Night Dragons.

"How many times must I say this? I am looking for TRUE stars, not bears and badgers and whatnot."

Suddenly, the little stars clinging to Stella's back let go and rose into the air. "We're true stars!" they cried. "We'll perform!"

They clustered together and darted toward the stage.

"Come back!" Stella called. She was sure that the junior stars should not perform. "You can't trust her!"

But the little stars didn't listen. To make matters worse, Fire Sparks began to buzz around Stella, attracted to her anger.

She swished at them with her tail and wings. By the time she'd cleared them away, it was too late. The little stars were up onstage, standing in neat rows. They glowed so brightly that Stella saw something she had not noticed before. Behind the stage was a huge metal cage. Inside, packed tightly, were more stars! They were much bigger than the little stars onstage. And they were much paler. It was like all their twinkly joy had been drained out of them, like light bulbs that were almost all used up.

LuckyStar fluttered up and down in distress. "The missing stars!"

Stella nodded. "The talent quest must be the Fire Queen's way of trapping even the smallest little stars from the forest!"

"Why would she do it?" Phoebe asked, looking sadly at the little stars about to perform.

"Maybe she uses their starlight to make herself brighter," Stella suggested.

LuckyStar stopped midair. "That actually makes sense. Starlight is one of the most powerful forms of energy in the forest."

Stella turned to her friends. "We have to stop them from performing," she said.

Rosie and Phoebe did not even bother replying. With firm nods, the three dragons rose into the air. But as they flew toward the stage, a wall of Fire Sparks blocked their way.

"You may not pass!" the Fire Queen cried. "Let the little stars perform!"

"Get off the stage!" Stella called to the little stars.

But they had already begun to dance. They twinkled their points and sang in their sweet, tinkly voices. Stella sighed. The little stars loved performing so much, they had fallen right into the Fire Queen's trap.

As the Dragon Girls watched, the cage behind the stage slowly lifted up as more Fire Sparks appeared. The Fire Sparks began tumbling around one another, picking up speed until they were a giant tornado of sparks. Slowly, they moved toward the little stars.

"Look behind you! Fly away!" Stella, Rosie, and Phoebe yelled at the stars, but the buzzing from the Fire Sparks was so loud, their voices were drowned out.

It was no good. The spark-nado closed in around the stars, catching them in its fury and dragging them into the cage.

Then, with a loud clang, the cage door slammed shut.

Fury coursed through Stella. "Let them out at once!" she demanded. "And the other stars you have in there, too!"

The Fire Queen just laughed.

Stella looked around at the crowd of forest creatures. They were all gazing calmly at the Fire Queen. Why weren't they reacting to what she had just done? Weren't they shocked to see the little stars trapped in a cage?

"They can't see what's happening," LuckyStar explained to Stella. "Only you and the other Night Dragons have strong enough vision to see what's truly going on. Everyone else is too dazzled by the Fire Queen."

The Fire Queen called out to Stella. "If you want to rescue the stars, you'll need to get up onstage and perform for me."

"She's lying!" Rosie growled.

Phoebe agreed. "There's no way she is going to release the stars. She is clearly using their energy for herself."

Stella knew her friends were right. "But if we

get up onstage, we'll at least be closer to the stars. That might give us a chance to rescue them."

Phoebe considered this. "It's a risk. But at least we'll be together. We can look out for one another."

The Fire Queen flared brighter than ever. She was already stealing energy from the little stars!

Swishing away the Fire Sparks that were clustered around her, Stella called out: "Very well. We will perform for you."

But the Fire Queen shook her head, her flaming hair leaving streaks in the air. "Only the Starlight Dragon may perform."

Phoebe looked at Stella, her eyes wide. "We can't let you go alone!" she cried.

"It's way too risky," Rosie agreed. "She will try and capture you, and steal your starlight."

Stella hesitated. It was almost certainly a trap. There was no way that the Fire Queen intended to play fair. But Stella also had a strong feeling, deep inside, that getting up on the stage was the right thing to do.

"Trust your feelings," murmured LuckyStar in her ear. "And don't forget that being angry can be powerful. You just need to channel it in the right way."

Stella gave each of her friends a quick wing

hug. "Don't worry," she told them. "I know what I'm doing. I think!"

Before she could change her mind, Stella flew up over the crowd and onto the floating stage. The forest animals clapped happily. They were all having a lovely time, with no idea of what was at stake.

"It'ssss a Night Dragon!" she heard a pink snake hiss to a bright green snake. "Thissss should be sssspecial."

Stella landed smoothly on the stage and turned to face the crowd. But deciding to go on the stage had been the easy part. Now that she was there, with all those eyes upon her,

Stella realized she had no idea what to do! She was confident, but performing had never been her thing. She wasn't a good singer. She didn't know any impressive dance moves. What could she do?

Then she heard a sound. It was a little whimper. A tinkling sort of whimper that was soon

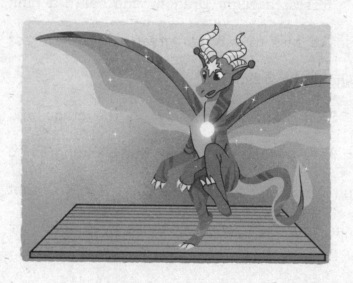

joined by others. Stella knew what the sound was. It was those poor little stars.

Stella had been trying to keep her anger contained. But this was too much! How could anyone lock up such tiny, twinkling stars? LuckyStar's words came back to her. *Being angry can be powerful. You just need to channel it in the right way.*

Yelling at the Fire Queen did not seem to make any difference. But maybe roaring would? This would not be a usual roar, though. This needed to be a roar that took all of Stella's outrage and turned it into something good and powerful.

Stella knew she had that kind of roar inside

her. She could feel it, bubbling deep in her chest. She breathed in deeply, feeling like she was drinking cool, clear water on a hot day. It reminded her of her strength.

What the Fire Queen is doing is wrong, she told herself. *And we Night Dragons are going to stop her.*

The roar began to build. It felt different somehow. It was clearly powerful, but it also felt more twinkly than usual. As she opened her mouth and roared, the air filled with tiny stars! The stars shimmered and bounced in the air. Then they began to grow bigger and brighter.

"Look out," Phoebe called from out in the crowd. "Fire Sparks are attacking!"

Sure enough, angry sparks zoomed toward her. But as they came closer, something happened. The sparks clashed in midair with Stella's star-filled roar. The Fire Sparks grew smaller and smaller until they disappeared. The roar-stars, on the other hand, continued to expand.

"Stop that at once!" the Fire Queen yelled. "You are stealing the energy from my Fire Sparks."

But Stella had no intention of stopping. She roared again, even more powerfully than before. As she did, Rosie and Phoebe flew over

and joined her onstage. Their faces were alight

with excitement.

"Look at the cage!" Phoebe cried.

The trapped stars were beginning to regain

their shine. They were filling out, too, no longer

looking as thin as paper. As they bloomed with

energy and hope, the bars of the cage began to groan with the strain.

It was a wonderful sight.

"It's going to break!" Rosie cheered, flapping her wings with joy.

The metal of the cage exploded into dust. The imprisoned stars burst free!

The sky blazed with starlight. Just moments ago it had been a dark, inky blue! Now stars zipped back and forth, squealing with star delight.

"The stars look better already," Phoebe said.

"They are much brighter," Rosie said, "but they're still not very shiny."

The stars looked a bit like old coins in need of a good polish. But at least they had lots of energy!

Down below, the creatures of the forest blinked and stretched. It was like they'd just woken from a deep sleep. The Fire Queen's hold over them was broken.

The animals chatted happily as they started to scurry, swim, or fly home. They were returning to their burrows, streams, and nests.

The Fire Queen, however, was not happy at all. She flew back and forth in a rage, her fiery gown trailing smoke behind her. She was trying to recapture the stars, but they were too quick for her. Each time, they slipped from her outstretched hands.

"Come back here!" she screamed, her voice so full of fury that she singed the leaves on a nearby tree. It wasn't very scary, though. She just wasn't as bright as before. She looked like a fire that was running out of fuel to burn.

The stars circled around her, blocking her way.

One of the bigger stars hovered above the others. It clapped two points together to get everyone's attention. "Follow me!" it called. "We need to get polished up so we can get the forest's wishes flowing again!"

The star took off like a rocket into the sky. Many of the other stars promptly shot off after it, leaving sparkly trails behind them.

"We should go, too," Stella said to her friends. "The Fire Queen will chase them as soon as she can. We need to make sure the stars get away safely."

"They're heading for the Wish Clouds," LuckyStar said as he cartwheeled over to Stella. "Those are the highest layer of clouds.

The air is too thin for dragons to fly that high. You'll need to catch a ride on a shooting star."

This sounded like an excellent idea to Stella! But catching a shooting star was easier said than done. Rosie was the first to do it. Phoebe and Stella cheered as she zoomed up into the dark sky. Then Phoebe took off, too. Stella was just about to catch one when she felt a tug on her wing. It was one of the little stars, and hovering next to it were all the other little stars.

"Can we ride with you?" the junior star asked. "We don't want to get lost."

"Of course," said Stella. "Climb on."

As the last little star clambered on, Stella saw a shooting star heading her way. It was a nice big one. Stella hoped it was strong enough to pull both a dragon and lots of little stars along.

It was! In fact, it was such a strong star that Stella soon caught up with Phoebe and Rosie. She could see on their faces that they were enjoying the ride just as much as she was.

"I wonder if this is what waterskiing feels like?" Phoebe called as her shooting star neatly dodged around other slower stars.

Rosie laughed. "If your boat was a star!"

Stella was having so much fun that she forgot all about the Fire Queen. It was only when she heard a crackling behind her that she turned and saw the Fire Queen's menacing shape. She was surrounded by sparks, but there were fewer of them than usual. She still looked a little scary, but there was no doubt the Fire Queen was weaker. And she looked furious about it!

Still, she was traveling fast, and gaining on the Night Dragons.

Stella felt the little stars on her back shiver nervously.

They flew through two layers of clouds before the shooting star they were riding called out, "Wish Clouds looming! Get ready for buffing!"

Up ahead was a layer of pale, silvery cloud. The stars all flew to it, disappearing into its billowing shapes.

Would they make it into the clouds before the queen reached them?

"I'm not finished with you yet!" the Fire Queen growled.

The queen loomed just behind Stella, one flaming hand reaching out to grab her tail.

"Well, we're finished with you!" Stella roared.

Rosie and Phoebe saw what was going on, and added their roars.

"Leave our friend alone!"

Their roars mingled and swirled with Stella's, shoving the Fire Queen back with a jolt. Stella felt energy surging through her. Right then, she was sure there was nothing she and her friends couldn't do together.

A moment later, Stella's shooting star flew into the Wish Clouds. Stella had expected it to be dark and gloomy in there, but it was quite the opposite. The clouds were all lit up by the stars flying through. They sparkled like a cave full of crystals.

"Ooooh!" cheered the little stars. "So pretty!"

It was pretty, and the clouds felt very soft and smooth as they brushed past Stella's skin. It was like being rubbed with the fluffiest towel imaginable.

All too soon they popped out the other side. But there was no time to be sad. The stars who had traveled through the cloud were gathered here. None of them were dull now. They were all polished to perfection. They floated in mid-air, admiring one another.

"We're so shiny," they cooed in delight.

"Everyone will want to wish on us now!"

The Night Dragons looked at one another. They were gleaming like metal. "We're shiny, too," Phoebe said.

"Maybe we could be stars!" Rosie laughed.

But Stella was too distracted to join in. The Fire Queen had been right behind her as she entered the Wish Cloud. Was she about to pop out the other side, too?

But no Fire Queen appeared. As Stella watched, a single Fire Spark drifted out of the Wish Cloud and hung in the air.

The magic thread on Stella's necklace was quick to react. It unraveled and lashed out.

"Whoa," Stella cried as the magic thread grabbed the tiny Fire Spark and wrapped itself around it to form a little cage.

"I didn't know it could do things like that!" Rosie gasped.

They watched as the thread retracted, pulling the trapped spark back to Stella.

Stella peered at it. Up close, she could see that it wasn't a Fire Spark at all. It was the Fire Queen herself! She had been shrunken. She was shaking her tiny fist at Stella, a furious look on her tiny face.

The mini Fire Queen looked almost cute, like a little angry ant.

Stella turned to the others, her eyes sparkling. "I don't think the Fire Queen is going to cause any more problems!"

At this news, the sky exploded with noise and movement. Stars zoomed through the sky, spinning and twirling and looping around one another. Some of them flashed different colors.

"It's like the most incredible fireworks display ever." Phoebe sighed.

"Exactly what I was thinking," Rosie agreed.

Stella felt a warmth spreading through her. At first she thought it was because she was so happy that they had succeeded in returning the stars to the sky.

But the feeling kept growing. And now Stella

could hear a sound, too. It was a faint whispering that seemed to be floating up from the forest below.

"That's all the wishes," LuckyStar explained as he spun gently closer. "The forest animals have started wishing again now that the stars are shining."

The stars swooped and danced through the whispering wishes. It was like they were collecting them up, growing steadily stronger and brighter as they did so.

Stella felt like she might explode from happiness. They had helped the creatures of the Magic Forest start to wish again. It was like a wish come true, all in itself!

LuckyStar did a cartwheel and landed on Stella's shoulder. "It's time to head back to the glade," he said. "The Tree Queen will want to see you."

Stella nodded. She loved watching the stars, but she was eager to see the queen again. "Ready?" she called to her friends.

"Sure," Rosie said, "but how will we get back down?"

Three stars promptly flew over. "We'll take you down. Grab on!"

"You can't leave without saying goodbye to us!" cried some tinkling little voices.

Stella, Phoebe, and Rosie were suddenly surrounded by junior stars.

"Have you guys grown?" Stella asked. They looked much bigger.

"Yes!" chattered the stars. "It's all the fresh air and big wishes. And guess what! We're allowed to stay up here to finish our training!"

"Well, make sure you keep twinkling," Stella said.

In response, the little stars twinkled furiously. They had definitely improved!

With their goodbyes said, the Night Dragons each grabbed the point of a star.

"Get ready to whoosh!" announced Stella's

star and, seconds later, they were hurtling through the star-studded sky and toward the treetops of the Magic Forest.

It was like diving into a deep pool of twinkling water. They were traveling so fast that Rosie and Phoebe were just blurs beside her, but Stella could hear them laughing and whooping.

As they got lower, Stella could saw countless animals gazing up at the sky. She knew just how they felt. Gazing up at the starry sky, wishing on the first star you saw ... and on the second, third, and fourth stars, too. It was the best thing ever!

I'm so glad we could return the stars to them, she thought as the shooting stars slowed to a hover above the treetops.

"You can fly from here," said the star Stella was holding.

"We sure can," said Stella, giving her star a quick thank-you hug.

"Hey!" Phoebe called, slowing to a stop beside her. "The glade is just down there." The force field glowed brightly. Starlight fell across it, making it twinkle.

LuckyStar left Stella's shoulder. "Goodbye," he said, bowing one of his points. "Thanks for granting my wish."

"Your wish?" Stella repeated.

LuckyStar did a twirl. "I've always dreamed of going on an adventure with a dragon," he said. "And now I have. Goodbye!"

Stella was sorry to see him go. Hopefully, one day she would see him again.

Stella turned to her friends. "Are we ready to land?" she asked, and the three friends flew lower and lower. Before they passed through the force field, Stella held her breath and made a wish.

A second later, she made a perfect landing inside the glade. Her wish had come true!

"Well done, Stella," said a warm and familiar voice.

The Tree Queen smiled broadly. "And well

done, all of you," she added, looking fondly at each of the three Night Dragons.

Stella took off the necklace and handed it to the Tree Queen. "Be careful," she warned. "The Fire Queen is trapped in that little cage made of thread."

The Tree Queen took the necklace in one of her long branch-arms. "Thank you," she said seriously. "We'll look after her. We all need fire, of course. But it must be controlled. I will try to ensure the Fire Queen and her sparks do not become too big or powerful again."

"I guess it's time to go," Rosie said sadly.

The Tree Queen rustled her leaves. "For now,

yes. But the Magic Forest will always be here, waiting for you."

Stella nodded, feeling sad and happy all at the same time.

Then Phoebe nudged her. "We have our midnight feast waiting for us back home."

She'd totally forgotten about their midnight feast! Yum!

They said farewell to the Tree Queen and pushed their way out through the force field. There, resting on the grass, was the bubble to take Stella back to the normal world. As she padded toward it, the bubble grew and grew, until it was big enough for her to walk through.

She closed her eyes and felt that wonderful swoosh!

When she opened her eyes again, she was back in her bedroom. Everything was the same as it had been. Except, were the stars outside the window just a little bit brighter?

A moment later, her bedroom door opened and her friends tiptoed in. Phoebe had juice, glasses, and plates. Rosie had a big bag of treats. They both grinned ear to ear, their eyes sparkling in the starlight that streamed through the window.

All of Stella's sad feelings about leaving the Magic Forest disappeared. Midnight feasts

were the best. And this time, they had their

biggest adventure yet to talk about!

Another clawsome series by the author of Dragon Girls!

Turn the page for a special sneak peek!

1

Lunchtime had arrived, but Luca was still in class. He had never been asked to stay back before. He didn't know why he had been asked to stay back today. Luca wasn't perfect but he didn't usually get into trouble.

On the blackboard, someone had scrawled a weird drawing. There was a shape that looked a bit like a crown. Another looked like a tooth.

To the side was something that looked like a fork. Around them all was a squiggly line. Luca was pretty sure Ms. Long had drawn it. But why? And what did it mean?

Ms. Long always did things her own way. Other kids learned English in English class. In history they did history. Ms. Long's classes weren't like that. In English, they might learn about riddles or codes. In history they might learn how to make arrows by chipping away at flint.

If Ms. Long could crack your code in less than five minutes, she would rip it up. If the tip of your arrow was not sharp enough to pierce thick cloth, she would toss the whole thing in the trash.

Lots of kids didn't like Ms. Long. They called her The Dragon. Some kids swore they'd seen smoke curl from her nostrils when she was upset.

But Luca thought she was interesting. He especially liked her stories. When she was in a good mood, Ms. Long told tales about an imaginary land called Imperia. Maybe she was writing a book or something? Luca didn't know and he didn't care. The stories were cool. Imperia had once been a beautiful place, filled with majestic mountains, endless forests and ancient cities that shone like gold. That was back when dragons were in charge.

But dark times had fallen on the realm. There

were no dragons left. The land was overrun with wild beasts and ruled by a power-hungry leader named Dartsmith. Ms. Long's Imperia stories always ended the same way.

"Only when the three dragons return will Imperia have peace again."

Luca looked back at the chalk drawing on the board. None of the other classrooms had blackboards. But Ms. Long's room was old-fashioned. One wall was completely covered with old display cases. These were made of carved wood and stained glass. Inside them were the sort of things you might find in a museum. Stuffed animals. Strange objects. Rocks.

Weirdly, it was the three rocks that always drew Luca's attention. One rock in particular, the one in the cabinet at the back of the classroom. It was the size and shape of a football.

Once, when she'd been in a surprisingly chatty mood, Ms. Long had taken it out of the cabinet.

"This is a geode," she had said, walking between the tables so everyone could see it up close. "Also known as a Thunder Egg. They are very rare. Thunder eggs look boring on the outside, but on the inside most of them are crystal. This one, however, is filled with something even more precious."

Luca wanted to touch the Thunder Egg. He

felt like the rock was calling to him. But there was no chance. Ms. Long returned it to the cabinet, locking it with her key.

Her good mood disappeared and she frowned at the class. "If any of you mess with this specimen," she said, "you will enter a *whole world* of trouble."

Now, sitting in the classroom waiting for Ms. Long to appear, Luca stared at the drawing. He stared so hard his eyes started to blur. The lines changed color. Now they looked gold, and not white at all.

"This is a total waste of time," snarled a voice.

Luca started. He'd forgotten he wasn't the only kid asked to stay back during lunch.

He turned to look at Zane, the class football champ. Zane's face was scrunched up and he was drumming his pencil on the table.

Ms. Long would have bitten his head off if she'd been around.

"Wow! Zane, you look soooo amazing right now."

This comment came from the third kid asked to stay back that afternoon. Yazmine. She had joined their class at the start of the year. Luca didn't know much about her. She kept to herself, her head always bent over her work.

Yazmine leaned back in her chair, smiling. Her green eyes were fixed on Zane.

Luca groaned. He could not work out why

Zane was so popular. Every boy wanted to be his friend. Every girl had his name written on their pencil-case. It made no sense. Zane was a total pain in the butt. He did what he wanted, with no worries about anyone else. Luca was pretty sure Zane didn't even know his name.

Zane was also one of those kids whose phone camera was permanently on selfie-mode.

He whipped out his phone now. "Really? I look amazing?" he asked, talking while trying to freeze his snarl.

Yazmine stood up and walked over to the blackboard. "Yeah. Amazingly stupid. Look, I don't know where Ms. Long has gone. But this," she pointed at the drawing, "must have some-thing to do with us being here. Let's figure it out so we can go eat."

Luca chuckled. This Yazmine was pretty cool.

Zane's frown deepened. "You'd better watch it, new girl."

"Firstly, I've been at this school for six months. I am hardly new," Yazmine retorted, hand on hip. "Secondly, what are you going to do? Pull out your comb and mess up my hair?"

Before Zane could respond, Yazmine turned to Luca. "Zane the Vain will be useless. But I bet you and I can work out what this draw-ing is. It's a kind of puzzle. You like puzzles, right?"

Luca stared at Yazmine in surprise. How did she know that?

"I guess," he mumbled. "But I don't have any idea what this is. Do you?"

Yazmine walked over to the board. "I think it's a map," she said, tracing the squiggly line with her finger. "Here's the coastline. And these shapes are landmarks. But the part I can't solve is what country it is."

Yazmine faced the board. Luca and Zane did the same, each tilting their heads to one side as they studied the drawing.

It suddenly dawned on Luca what he was looking at. As he said it aloud, so did Yazmine and Zane.

"Imperia!"

There was a clicking noise. The cabinet at the back of the classroom had somehow unlocked itself! The door swung slowly forward, like a ghost was opening it with an invisible hand. As Luca watched, he knew what was going to happen before it happened, almost like he'd dreamt it.

The Thunder Egg that was always displayed in the cabinet tipped forward. As they watched, it rolled to the edge of the shelf and started to fall. Zane sped across the room and dived toward it. He reached out and caught the egg just before it smashed to the floor.

Luca blinked. He hated to admit it, but that was impressive.

But then Zane pulled a typically Zane move. "Hey, you! Leo or whatever your name is," he called to Luca. "Catch!"

Fear pounded in Luca's chest. "Don't!" he yelled.

But it was too late. The Thunder Egg arced through the air toward him.

Luca leapt up, hands outstretched. As his fingers touched the egg, the classroom lights flickered. Once. Twice. There was a flash of purple. Then everything went black.

ABOUT THE AUTHORS

Maddy Mara is the pen name of Australian creative duo Hilary Rogers and Meredith Badger. Hilary and Meredith have been making children's books together for many years. They love dreaming up new ideas and always have lots of projects bubbling away. When not writing, Hilary can be found cooking weird things or going on long walks, often with Meredith. And Meredith can be found teaching English online all around the world or daydreaming about being able to fly. They both currently live in Melbourne, Australia. Their website is maddymara.com.

DRAGON GIRLS

THE GLITTER DRAGONS

DRAGON GIRLS

Azmina the Gold
Glitter Dragon

Maddy Mara

THE GLITTER DRAGONS

DRAGON GIRLS

Willa the Silver
Glitter Dragon

Maddy Mara

THE GLITTER DRAGONS

DRAGON GIRLS

Naomi the Rainbow
Glitter Dragon

Maddy Mara

THE TREASURE DRAGONS

DRAGON GIRLS

Mei the Ruby
Treasure Dragon

Maddy Mara

THE TREASURE DRAGONS

DRAGON GIRLS

Aisha the Sapphire
Treasure Dragon

Maddy Mara

THE TREASURE DRAGONS

DRAGON GIRLS

Quinn the Jade
Treasure Dragon

Maddy Mara

THE NIGHT DRAGONS

DRAGON GIRLS

Rosie the
Twilight Dragon

Maddy Mara

THE NIGHT DRAGONS

DRAGON GIRLS

Phoebe the
Moonlight Dragon

Maddy Mara

THE NIGHT DRAGONS

DRAGON GIRLS

Stella the
Starlight Dragon

Maddy Mara

Collect them all!